This book belongs to...

Name:..

Age:..

Published by Dennis Lifestyle Ltd. 30 Cleveland St, London W1T 4JD. Company registered in England.

Don't worrry! We'll protect you from him!

MINECRAFT SECRETS & CHEATS

CONTENTS

64 HOW TO BE A MINECRAFT EXPERT

MEET STEVE & ALEX!

As we're going to be talking about Minecraft, let's meet the two leading characters in the game. After all, at first, you'll be looking a lot like Steve or Alex!

Steve

Introduced in the very early version of Minecraft in December 2010, Steve was the only default skin for almost four years. Named by Minecraft's creator Notch, it's often written as "Steve?" because Notch wasn't sure if that was his official name! Steve has blue eyes and brown hair, and wears a light blue T-shirt, blue jeans and grey shoes. The original version had a brown goatee beard! Steve has appeared as a playable character in Super Meat Boy and Retro City Rampage. He's also a micromob in various LEGO Minecraft sets.

Alex

Alex was added to Minecraft in August 2014. She isn't in all versions, but you can currently choose her on the PC and console editions. She has green eyes and ginger hair in a ponytail. She wears a green tunic with a belt, brown leggings and grey boots. Her character model has thinner arms than Steve, but this is the only difference between the two. Alex hasn't appeared in other games yet, but her micromob will be included in two Minecraft LEGO sets – The Desert Outpost and The Nether Fortress.

101 THINGS YOU NEVER KNEW ABOUT MINECRAFT

1

A cactus in a flower pot is harmless

Let's start with a simple one! Did you know that as well as flowers and ferns, flower pots also accept cacti? Place a cactus block inside and it turns into a small, harmless cactus!

2

Build your base in a mountain for easy resources and protection

If you build your base in the side of a mountain, there'll be fewer ways for mobs to sneak up on you. You'll also get easy access to coal and iron, both of which form above ground inside mountains!

3

Netherrack never goes out

Once you set Netherrack on fire, it keeps burning until deliberately put out. Even rain won't affect it! You can use this trick to create fireplaces or dramatic-looking lights.

4

Water source blocks flow towards the edges of a block – or all four if it's open on all sides!

Water source blocks automatically flow towards the edge of any block they're placed on top of, so you can use this knowledge to direct the flow of them in the direction you want.

5

Grass doesn't grow on podzol!

Podzol is a special type of dirt found only in mega taiga biomes. You can collect it only if you have a shovel with the silk touch enchantment. It keeps mushrooms alive in direct sunlight!

6

This baby rabbit is of no use to anyone, although it does look cute!

Baby animals don't drop anything when they die, so don't kill them! Leave them alone until they become adults. You don't even get experience for your kill if they aren't fully grown.

7

Emerald ore only forms underground near the extreme hills biome

Emerald ore is very rare in Minecraft, and it can only be found in or near an extreme hills biome. It only appears deep underground, in similar places to gold and diamond.

8

I don't fancy this chicken's chances

Packs of wolves will hunt for other animals, such as chickens, sheep and rabbits. However, the good news is that they won't attack you in the game unless you hit one of them first.

9

Lava flows faster and further in the Nether

In the Nether, lava flows more quickly and for a longer distance than in the Overworld, so you've got even less time to get out of the way of it if you accidentally mine a hole it can get through!

10

Baa baa grey sheep...

If you breed two sheep of a different colour, its wool will be a mix of the two. If the colours can't be mixed, the baby sheep will randomly copy the colour of one parent.

11

A rabbit called Toast gets a unique skin!

You can use nametags to give mobs unique names, and some special names unlock secret Easter eggs. Try naming a rabbit "Toast", a sheep "jeb_" and any mob either "Dinnerbone" or "Grumm".

12

Coal, granite, andesite and diorite can all generate above ground

If you don't want to risk going underground, you can find coal and iron above ground in mountain biomes. Just look for exposed stone and you're guaranteed to find a few blocks.

13

Unlike torches, glowstone works underwater

Lighting underwater is difficult, but glowstone blocks, redstone lamps, Jack 'o' lanterns and sea lanterns all emit the highest possible light level and, unlike torches, they can be placed underwater.

14

Huge mushrooms can generate in and around certain forests

Every block of a huge mushroom has the chance of dropping 0-2 mushrooms when it is broken. The quickest way to do this is with an axe, but in truth, any tool should work fine.

15

Carpet lets you climb over fences

Fences are a block and a half tall to stop players and mobs jumping over them, but if you place a piece of carpet on top of a fence it will allow you to jump over it. Only rabbits can get in and out the same way.

16

Snow falls in cold biomes, carpeting exposed blocks with snow

Rain falls as snow in cold biomes. What's more, snowfall leaves a layer of snow on top of any exposed blocks, which you can collect as snowballs! You just need to use a spade to do so.

17

The moon's phases have an effect on mobs

The moon's phases affect how mobs spawn. You see more slimes on the surface of swamp biomes when it's full, and it can increase the chance of mobs spawning with status effects and enchanted weapons.

18

Forest hills biomes are tricky to navigate

Some biomes can spawn as hilly variants. Forest hills biomes are hard to navigate, but if you get up high it makes it easy to see what's around and spot any enemies who might try to sneak up on you!

19

Cocoa beans growing on a jungle tree

Cocoa pods grow naturally on jungle trees, but you can also farm cocoa beans by "planting" them on a tree trunk. They grow into full-size pods and you can then collect more cocoa beans from them.

20

This map helps you figure out where you are in the world

When you've made a map of an area, place it in an item frame on the wall so that you can see it. The location of the map is marked on it by a green blob so that you can find yourself.

21

Lightning can create witches

Lightning has some weird effects. A villager struck by lightning turns into a witch, a pig turns into a zombie pigman, and a creeper turns into a super-explosive charged creeper!

22

Slime blocks are really useful, if you can get enough slimeballs to make them!

Slime blocks can be created by crafting nine slimeballs together. They slow down anything that walks on them and, if you jump on top of one from high up, you don't take any damage and bounce back up!

23

Red mushrooms underground

Mushrooms are one of the few plants that can grow underground. They need dirt and a low level of light to survive, so under the right conditions – usually if lava's nearby – you can find them deep underground.

24

I'm sure there's enough to go around...

You can make animals follow you by holding certain types of food. Chickens will follow you if you're holding grass seeds, for example. You can then use this behaviour to pen in animals for farming.

25

Rain, rain, go away...

Rainstorms block out the sun, and the darkened light levels allow enemy mobs to spawn and interfere with daylight sensors. If you don't want it to keep raining, you can sleep in a bed to skip it!

26

Flower forests are crammed with different types of flower. Stock up!

Flower forests contain several unique types of flower, so remember to stock up whether you're looking for some decorative plants others won't have or just want to collect all of the dye colours.

27

Several squid in a small pool

Squid will spawn in a pool of water, so be on the lookout. It's easier to collect the experience and ink sacs they drop if you don't have to swim a lot. Killing squid in the ocean makes their drops hard to find.

28

You should've seen the one that got away!

If you want to stock up on hunger-eliminating meat but can't find any farm animals, remember that you can fish in almost any amount of water. Don't eat the pufferfish, though – you'll get poisoned!

29

A new lava flow setting a forest alight

Lava doesn't flow until its chunk gets loaded, so the first time you find a lava lake or flow above ground it may start a forest fire! Don't worry about stopping it – it should burn out naturally if you leave it.

30

Iron armour looks impressive and is very strong, but doesn't enchant easily

Armour will protect you from most physical attacks, but not from fire, drowning or falling. Luckily, there are enchantments you can add to each type of armour to reduce these effects too!

31

Get your head above the clouds in savanna plateau biomes

Savanna plateaus are already tall, but there's a mountainous variant – savanna plateau M – which is the only biome in the game where the terrain stretches high above the clouds.

32

Saplings make an inefficient fuel, but are easy to obtain in a pinch

If you don't have any coal handy, remember that you can use lots of things as fuel for a furnace, including crafted wood and plants and saplings. They might not burn for long, but it gets the job done!

33

Biomes usually keep to themselves

The colour of plants changes based on the temperature of the biome you're in. It's often easy to spot a biome's boundary because the grass and trees will change to a different shade of green.

34

Use Jack 'o' lanterns to light dark areas

Although they look a bit scary, Jack 'o' Lanterns emit the highest level of light, along with glowstone and sea lanterns, with the added benefit that they're easier to get hold of than either of those blocks.

CONTINUED ON PAGE 26

15

17

Minecraft MONSTER Guide

Read on, ye seasoned adventurer, and learn of the dangerous beasts and monsters of Minecraft

NAME: Blaze
LOCATION: Nether fortresses
DROPS: Blaze rod (PC)/glowstone dust (console)

Dangerous creatures of the Nether that often appear in groups. Their fireballs are inaccurate but fast, and you'll get burned if you get close to one. They also fly if they need to!

NAME: Cave spider
LOCATION: Abandoned mineshafts
DROPS: String, spider eye

Cave spiders are slightly smaller than their cousins and have a bluer sheen. Similar to normal spiders, these arachnids can climb walls and won't attack in light. However, they only spawn deep underground. Their bite can poison the unwary.

NAME: Chicken jockey
LOCATION: Rare appearances in dark areas
DROPS: Feathers, raw chicken, rotten flesh, rarely carrots, potatoes, iron ingots

A tiny zombie riding a chicken. Despite looking ridiculous, they're very fast and their weak attacks can quickly do serious damage to you. You've been warned!

NAME: Creeper
LOCATION: Wherever you least expect them
DROPS: Gunpowder

Minecraft's most famous monster. Probably behind you right now! Self-destructs, destroying unwary players and all their hard work.

NAME: Elder guardian
LOCATION: Underwater, ocean monuments
DROPS: Prismarine crystals, prismarine shards, raw fish

Tough, dangerous sea creatures that defend ocean monuments. Engage with caution. Elder guardians don't respawn. For more, see Guardian.

NAME: Enderman
LOCATION: Low light areas
DROPS: Ender pearl

Endermen aren't dangerous unless you look directly at them. If you do, they'll immediately teleport towards you and attack! They're otherwise harmless, passively moving blocks.

NAME: Endermite
LOCATION: Spawned by players
DROPS: Nothing

Endermites are small, weak creatures that may spawn when an ender pearl is used to teleport. Endermen will attack endermites.

NAME: Ghast
LOCATION: The Nether, often near lava lakes
DROPS: Gunpowder, ghast tear

Ghasts are huge ghosts that spit fireballs. They can do a lot of damage, but are easy to kill with a bow and arrow.

NAME: Guardian
LOCATION: Underwater, ocean monuments
DROPS: Prismarine crystals, prismarine shards, raw fish

Be wary of attacking guardians when their spines are extended. To avoid their laser beams, dodge behind blocks. Watch out for their more deadly cousins, the elder guardians.

21

NAME: Magma cube
LOCATION: Anywhere in the Nether, especially fortresses
DROPS: Magma cream

Magma cubes vary in size, and destroying larger cubes may spawn smaller ones, much like slimes. Try not to touch them as they're hot!

NAME: Silverfish
LOCATION: Underground, monster eggs or strongholds
DROPS: Nothing

Small critters that hide in stone blocks, converting them to monster eggs. Will attack if startled and can summon other Silverfish.

NAME: Skeleton
LOCATION: Low light areas, Nether fortresses
DROPS: Bones, arrows and maybe weapons they're using

Common monsters that attack from range with a bow or up close with a sword. Not too dangerous, but beware of arrows knocking you off ledges!

NAME: Spider jockey
LOCATION: Low light areas
DROPS: Bones, arrows, skeleton's weapons, string, spider eyes

Rare, less ridiculous than chicken jockeys and can actually prove dangerous! The spider drives; the skeleton's just along for the ride. A wither skeleton riding a cave spider can ruin your day!

NAME: Spider
LOCATION: Low light areas
DROPS: String, spider eye

Along with skeletons, creepers and zombies, spiders are the most common enemies. They can climb walls, so high ground isn't always safe. They won't attack in well-lit areas.

NAME: Slime
LOCATION: Underground, swamps at night
DROPS: Slimeball (tiny slimes only)

Slimes sound disgusting, but aren't too dangerous. Slaying larger slimes may spawn smaller slimes, however, so beware of getting outnumbered!

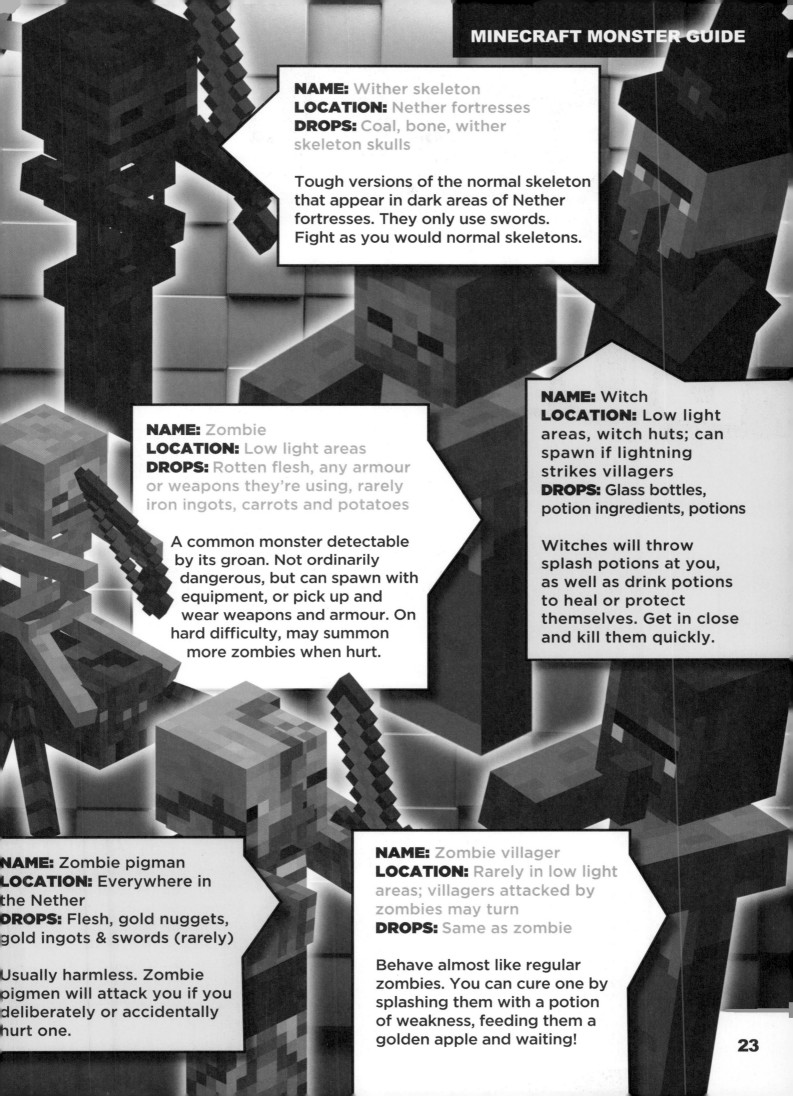

NAME: Wither skeleton
LOCATION: Nether fortresses
DROPS: Coal, bone, wither skeleton skulls

Tough versions of the normal skeleton that appear in dark areas of Nether fortresses. They only use swords. Fight as you would normal skeletons.

NAME: Zombie
LOCATION: Low light areas
DROPS: Rotten flesh, any armour or weapons they're using, rarely iron ingots, carrots and potatoes

A common monster detectable by its groan. Not ordinarily dangerous, but can spawn with equipment, or pick up and wear weapons and armour. On hard difficulty, may summon more zombies when hurt.

NAME: Witch
LOCATION: Low light areas, witch huts; can spawn if lightning strikes villagers
DROPS: Glass bottles, potion ingredients, potions

Witches will throw splash potions at you, as well as drink potions to heal or protect themselves. Get in close and kill them quickly.

NAME: Zombie pigman
LOCATION: Everywhere in the Nether
DROPS: Flesh, gold nuggets, gold ingots & swords (rarely)

Usually harmless. Zombie pigmen will attack you if you deliberately or accidentally hurt one.

NAME: Zombie villager
LOCATION: Rarely in low light areas; villagers attacked by zombies may turn
DROPS: Same as zombie

Behave almost like regular zombies. You can cure one by splashing them with a potion of weakness, feeding them a golden apple and waiting!

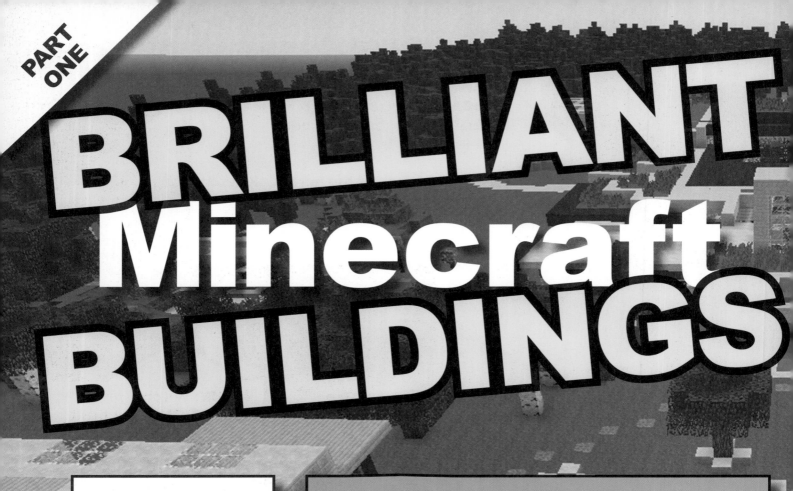

BRILLIANT Minecraft BUILDINGS

If you're more of a builder than a fighter, why not use Creative mode to let your imagination run free? All maps are available to download from **www.minecraftmaps. com**. Ask a parent before you download any, though!

STADIUM (SPORT CENTER)
Built by Brazilian Leonardo Maronez in advance of his country's Olympic Games, this custom map features a football stadium, Olympic-sized swimming pool and a gymnasium! Built completely to scale and with some impressive detailing. Check out the scoreboards and the player exits leading to changing rooms!

The resort lounge

THE RESORT
Created by mjin79, The Resort is a huge holiday complex where all is not as it seems. Filled with hidden rooms, special commands and signs to help you explore, there's more to this building than there first seems. Just don't complain about the room you're assigned when you check in!

The whole resort complex

ARBOREAL

Built by a user named SwitchB0ard, Arboreal is a strange floating world where everyone lives on islands floating in the sky. The inhabitants of the world mostly build their homes inside a giant tree that grows from the bottom of the world and stretches to the very top. You could spend hours exploring this fascinating world. Find hidden homes, a marketplace, hot air balloons and more, all hidden inside a strange, centuries-old tree.

The tree from the very bottom

A bazaar marketplace within the tree itself

There are sets for all environments

Hot air balloons provide access to inhabitants

A projection room for testing prints

THE MOVIE STUDIO

This build is based on a classic Hollywood movie studio and was created by David Thorpe as a tribute to that era. Inside you'll find studios, sets and stages for all kinds of movie scenes, an empty studio for you to build a set in yourself, and there's even a fun trail to follow exploring the mystery of the movie studio phantom. And, of course, there's a secret room to look for!

The outside of the studios. Looks inviting!

CONTINUED ON PAGE 40

25

101 THINGS YOU NEVER KNEW ABOUT MINECRAFT

35

Get out of the rain by entering a desert!

When it rains in Minecraft, it rains everywhere in your world at the same time. The only place you're safe is in hotter biomes like deserts and savanna, where it never rains at all.

36

This minecraft train can transport two full crates and one player!

If you put a powered minecart at either end of a line, you can create a "train" of several minecarts that can transport items from one place to another. Remember to leave an empty cart for you to ride in!

37

Naming a mob prevents it from despawning

Captain Kirk

Using a nametag on a mob in Minecraft keeps it in your world until it dies. You can even keep enemy mobs around if you want to – just don't set the difficulty to Peaceful!

38

Stay away from witch huts unless you're ready for a fight

Be careful if you come across a witch hut in a swamp. Witches can come out in the day and throw potions at you, which might make it hard for you to survive a fight unless you've come prepared!

39

Build a beacon to get the final achievement

The final achievement requires you to build a beacon. Once you've done this, there's nothing else left to do in the game (yet!). You have to defeat the wither to reach this point, so it might take a while!

40

You can grow a huge mushroom yourself!

Turn a normal mushroom into a huge mushroom by fertilising it with bone meal. This only works if there's enough space. If the light levels are high, you'll need to use more bone meal than if the light is low.

41

A redstone block emitting a charge

Redstone blocks can be used to store redstone, but they also emit an always-on redstone charge. This is useful, as you can use it then as part of redstone circuits.

42

Take care - you don't want to lose those diamonds!

The way diamonds spawn means they have a high chance of appearing near lava. Take care when you mine these blocks, as the lava will incinerate a dropped diamond before you have a chance to collect it!

43

Use iron bars in your windows to make arrow slits

Iron bars make a great alternative to windows because you can fire arrows through them. This means you can create arrow slits for defence without worrying about mobs firing back at you.

44

Monster spawners are risky to attack, but the rewards are huge

Monster spawners give you loads of experience if you destroy them, but they can be hard to find. The best way is to follow the shallow caves that generate in the surface.

45

The killer bunny is a white rabbit with bright red eyes. If you get too close, it attacks players and even wolves! Watch out if you see one – they're rare, but vicious!

46

The rabbit's foot is lucky for you, but not for the rabbit!

Roughly one in every 40 rabbits killed by you will drop a rabbit's foot, which you can then use to create a potion of leaping if you brew it with an awkward potion.

47

Soul sand and slabs can trap any mob

Soul sand sticks any player or mob to the ground, so you can trap them by surrounding soul sand with slabs. It's a great way to capture mobs for taming or farming, and to slow down players.

48

Large herds can be thinned out a little

If you come across a herd of animals, don't kill all of them even if you need food. If you leave two animals alive, the herd can breed back into a larger one. Leave one (or none) alive and it's gone for good!

49

Sunflowers always face the sun

Sunflowers usually can only be found on sunflower plains (unless they're replanted somewhere else), but wherever they're planted they'll always face the sun.

50

Melons in the jungle

Melons only grow naturally in jungle biomes, where you can find them on the floor in patches. Craft them into melon seeds and you can grow them anywhere if you've got dirt and water handy!

51

Lily pads crossing a river

Lily pads only appear in swampland, but you can collect and place them on top of any water. This is useful because players and mobs can walk on top of them, meaning you can create a simple bridge.

52

The elusive chiselled sandstone!

Desert temples are the only place to find chiselled sandstone blocks and smooth sandstone blocks, making up the pillars surrounding the central chamber. Faster than crafting from regular sandstone!

53

This chicken is heading home to roost – in style!

Minecarts can contain a lot of things and you can even ride one yourself. You can also force mobs to ride in minecarts by pushing them into an empty one. They'll only be able to get out if you release them.

54

Water, water, everywhere

Boats are incredibly quick when they get up to full speed. If you're exploring or mapping an area and there's water nearby, it makes sense to hop in a boat rather than lumber your way across the hills!

55

Put a clock in an item frame to make a wall clock

Simply place a clock inside an item frame and then you create a wall clock. A wall clock allows you to see what time of day it is without having to waste a slot in your inventory!

56

A snow golem. Creepy!

Snow golems leave a trail of snow wherever they walk, so you can generate one in a pit and it will create an infinite amount of snow for you to collect. Now if only there was a good use for it!

YOU'LL FIND PART THREE ON PAGE 50!

HAVE YOU TRIED THESE MINECRAFT RECIPES?

Learning all of the recipes in Minecraft can take forever, and some are difficult without help! Here are some recipes and crafting combinations that you might not have tried

FOOD

Controlling your hunger is a constant battle, so learning the different food types you can craft is essential for keeping up your health!

CAKES are food blocks you make out of sugar, milk, eggs and wheat. You have to place them before you can eat any, so it's a good way to store food! Each slice restores one full unit of your hunger bar, and there are seven slices in a cake.

You can craft eight **COOKIES** out of two wheat and one cocoa bean. What's more, each single cookie restores one full unit of hunger. The main benefit of cookies in the game is that they restore only a small amount of hunger, so you don't really waste anything if you eat one while you're already nearly full!

Mushrooms are easy to find in Minecraft, but the downside is that they can't be eaten on their own. You can craft them with a bowl to create **MUSHROOM STEW**, which restores three full units of hunger and leaves you the bowl to reuse. You can also milk mooshrooms (cows found in mushroom island biomes) with a bowl to fill it up with stew!

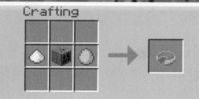

SECRET ITEMS

RABBIT STEW restores five hunger units for each one you eat. You make it by crafting together a bowl, a baked potato, a carrot, a cooked rabbit and a mushroom of any colour. Separately, the ingredients restore more hunger, but rabbit stew uses less inventory space!

Crafting a pumpkin together with an egg and sugar allows you to create **PUMPKIN PIE,** which restores four full units of hunger. This is a straightforward one, too. You can find all of the ingredients easily in the wild and there's no need to wait for it to cook!

There are lots of items in Minecraft that you can't find or buy, and can only make if you know how. Here are some that you might not have heard of!

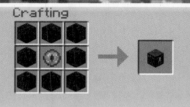

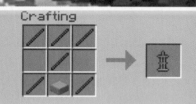

Use a crafting table to surround one eye of ender with eight obsidian to create an **ENDER CHEST**. Each chest leads to the same storage area, so you can carry items a long way.

Created from six sticks and a stone slab, **ARMOUR STANDS** can be used to display armour, mob heads and pumpkins. They're mostly just for decoration!

Did you know it's possible to create fireballs? If you craft blaze powder, coal (or charcoal) and gunpowder together, you'll create three **FIRE CHARGES**.

When you kill a slime, you can collect slimeballs, which can be crafted as part of leads, magma cream and sticky pistons. You can also craft together nine slimeballs to make a **SLIME BLOCK**. They slow down mobs and players.

Beacons fire a beam of light up into the air. To create one, place a **BEACON BLOCK** on top of a pyramid of iron, gold, diamond or emerald. To create a beacon block, craft five glass, a Nether star and three obsidian.

Decorative Blocks

Most of these decorative blocks can't be found in the Overworld, but they're simple to create and fun to use!

If you surround any piece of dye (or an object that acts as dye, like cocoa beans) with hardened clay blocks or glass blocks, you can create **STAINED GLASS AND STAINED CLAY**, which is useful for creating different forms of decoration around your world. Stained clay can be found in small amounts in desert temples and in huge amounts in the very rare mesa biome, but stained glass has to be crafted.

You can create a basic **BANNER** using six wool (of any colour) and one stick. Once you've made a banner, it's then possible to add up to six extra patterns to decorate it, meaning there are hundreds of combinations available! Banners are great for staking your claim to different territories in a multiplayer world, so why not create a signature design of your own?

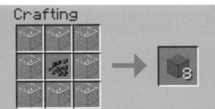

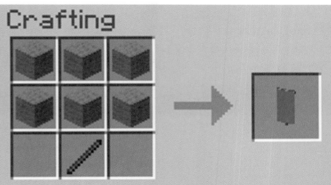

A recent update to Minecraft added several new types of common **STONE** – diorite, andesite and granite – and new crafting recipes to accompany them. You can turn cobblestone into diorite by crafting two blocks with two pieces of Nether quartz. You can change diorite into polished diorite by crafting four blocks together.

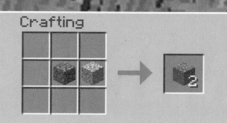

You can make two andesite blocks by combining one diorite block with one cobblestone block. You can also turn andesite into polished andesite by crafting four blocks together. You can make granite by crafting diorite with a piece of Nether quartz, and you can make polished granite by crafting four blocks together.

Structures

Although there are places where you can find certain structures, some can be found only by building them yourself!

WALLS act like fences, but don't appear naturally. You can make six wall or mossy wall blocks out of six cobblestone or six mossy cobblestone. Like fences, players and mobs can't jump over walls. They're better at keeping mobs away than two cobblestone blocks on top of one another, but skeletons can shoot over them more easily!

Crafted from two wooden planks with two sticks either side, **FENCE GATES** are half door, half fence. They can be opened and closed like doors, but can't be jumped over like fences. They can be controlled by redstone power. If you place a fence gate next to a wall or fence, they'll connect up to them, but not to glass panes or iron railings.

You can make a **REDSTONE LAMP** by crafting a glowstone block with four pieces of redstone dust. The lamp that results looks similar to glowstone, but its light can be activated and deactivated by a redstone charge. When active, a redstone lamp produces a light level of 15, which is the most any block can produce in the game.

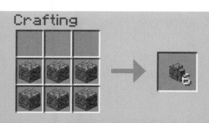

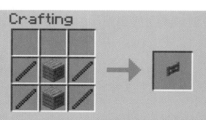

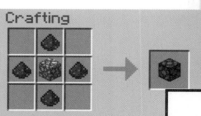

THE MINECRAFT TIMELINE

At the start of 2009, Minecraft didn't exist. Just over five years later, it's one of the biggest and best video games in the world. Here's the history of the game!

MAY 2009
Markus 'Notch' Persson starts working on what he then calls 'Cave Game'. Within days, he changes its name to Minecraft. The first test release of the game – Version 0.0.11a – arrives on 17th May.

JUNE 2009
The first multiplayer version of Minecraft is released.

DECEMBER 2009
As the game continues to develop, it now costs a small amount of money to play. It's still a bargain though!

JUNE 2010
Minecraft sells its 20,000th account. The price of a game account goes up!

AUGUST 2010
Multiplayer Survival mode is released for the first time.

OCTOBER 2010
Mojang is founded, the company that publishes Minecraft.

DECEMBER 2010
The near-finished beta release of Minecraft is released.

JANUARY 2011
Sales of Minecraft accounts pass 1 million!

MAY 2011
Minecraft Pocket Edition is announced for the first time. Soon, iPad and iPhone users will get the game!

JUNE 2011
Mojang reveals that Minecraft is coming to the Xbox 360! Lots of skins will follow (see page 84!).

AUGUST 2011
The first test version of Minecraft Pocket

The very first version of Minecraft!

Edition is released. An iPad version follows in November.

JANUARY 2012

The first LEGO Minecraft set is confirmed! We love the LEGO Minecraft sets!

MAY 2012

Minecraft is released for the Xbox 360 console.

JUNE 2012

The first LEGO Minecraft set is released! More will follow, and we'll buy them all!

APRIL 2013

Minecraft 2 is announced, but it turns out to be an April Fool's joke! Maybe one day...

JUNE 2013

Minecraft is announced for the Xbox One.

AUGUST 2013

Mojang confirms the PlayStation 3, PlayStation 4 and PlayStation Vita versions of Minecraft as well!

DECEMBER 2013

The beta version of Minecraft Realms is released!

SEPTEMBER 2014

By now, Minecraft on the PC is up to version 1.8!

SEPTEMBER 2014

Microsoft buys Mojang for – wait for it! – $2,500,000,000! Imagine all the yummy sweets you can buy with that!

NOVEMBER 2014

Notch leaves Mojang. Awwww....

MAY 2015

Minecraft is now up to version 1.8.6! The brilliant updates just keep on coming!

DECEMBER 2015

More people than ever get Minecraft goodies for Christmas! Good old Santa!

THE BEST MINECRAFT YOUTUBE CHANNELS

Minecraft is the most popular game on YouTube, and there are loads of channels out there covering all things blocky. Here's our pick of the best and most popular channels

THE DIAMOND MINECART
www.youtube.com/user/
TheDiamondMinecart

Riding along in the Diamond Minecart is DanTDM, aka Daniel, a British YouTuber and pug owner! Awww. I wonder if different dog breeds will ever be added to Minecraft?

He publishes at least one new Minecraft video every day, and usually more! These include reviews of cool new mods and maps, as well as multi-episode adventure stories.

A recurrent Diamond Minecart character is the troublesome Dr Trayaurus, who is prone to getting himself mixed up in unusual adventures. DanTDM usually has to fix Trayaurus's messes, but somehow the pesky doctor hasn't been fired yet!

Well... if you insist, Dr Trayaurus

Pull that lever there..

STAMPYLONGHEAD
www.youtube.com/user/
stampylonghead

Another Brit and daily updater, Stampy is upbeat and cheerful. Rather than reviewing mods and playing mini-games, he tells ongoing stories.

Stampy mostly plays the Xbox version of Minecraft, and his Let's Play series includes over 300 videos, so you can imagine how grand his survival world has become!

Stampy also runs occasional spin-offs, like episodes where he runs through adventure maps with his friends.

A minecart rollercoaster inside a giant creeper? I'm... scared!

SKY DOES MINECRAFT
www.youtube.co.uk/user/
skydoesminecraft

American Sky is the most popular Minecraft YouTuber in the world right now, putting out at least one video a day.

His videos often involve him and his friends playing mini-games or trying out Minecraft mods, but he also releases short machinima films and comedy skits.

Sky's subscribers are called the Sky Army and join him in hating Squid and loving Butter (aka Gold). He may not be for everyone, but with over 11 million subscribers the Sky Army is getting pretty big!

Sky's most-watched video is a parody of Coldplay's song 'Paradise'

Yogscast have released original songs, such as 'Diggy Diggy Hole'

AND I'M DIGGING A HOLE

YOGSCAST LEWIS & SIMON
www.youtube.com/user/
BlueXephos

Also known as BlueXephos and Honeydew, Brits Lewis and Simon are the Yogscast founders and two of the earliest Minecraft successes on YouTube.

While they started out talking about their experiences playing Minecraft and introducing thousands of new players to the game via a Let's Play, today their videos focus on comedy and Minecraft mods, mini-games and maps.

Yogscast has expanded a lot since 2010 and, despite their popularity booming through Minecraft, today Simon, Lewis and their recruits cover a wide variety of different games.

THE BEST
OMG!
MINECRAFT MOMENTS

We love Minecraft so much because it's full of moments of wonder, beauty, terror, excitement and joy. Moments that make us think "OMG"! Like these...

FIRST NIGHT

This is an experience that everyone who has played Minecraft will remember: surviving their first night.

Okay, this sounds like a boring choice to start with. But then think back: you probably spent your first day in Minecraft figuring out what you could do, then running around having fun. When it began getting dark and monsters appeared, you panicked (at least a little).

So you crafted a simple shelter, or just hid in a hole until the nasty, dangerous things went away. It was dark and scary, and you had no torches.

But after long minutes of terror had passed, and the sun began to rise once again, you realised you'd survived! Phew!

Yes, this seems like a safe place to bed down for the night

It goes on forever!

GOING DEEPER UNDERGROUND

The best way to find the coolest stuff is to keep exploring caves until you find one that goes on and on and on.

I'VE MADE A TERRIBLE MISTAKE

So you've spent so long underground that you no longer have any idea whether it's day or night up above.

You've used lots of torches exploring endless tunnels, and broken half a dozen pickaxes mining stacks of precious minerals. Then everything goes wrong!

Maybe you weren't paying attention for a few seconds, or never even noticed that hole in the cave roof. Whatever happened, something surprised or attacked you, and you fell into lava.

All you can think is: "If only I'd remembered to bring a bucket of water"!

At first, you remember every twist and turn you've explored, everything you've dug up and defeated. Then you step into a new area and everything suddenly changes.

Perhaps because all you can see is a huge cavern, stretching out into the darkness, lit only by orange lava falls. Perhaps because you've found the traces of an abandoned mineshaft – rails, cobwebs, ancient torches – or encountered something even rarer.

Whatever it is, it's a special moment that belongs entirely to you!

No, no, no, this isn't what I meant to do!

AH, THAT'S HOW FIRE WORKS

On the subject of unpleasant burning: think back to the first time you started a fire in Minecraft. Now think back to the first time you built something out of wood.

These two things were probably related in a way that you later wished they weren't. That was just cruel!

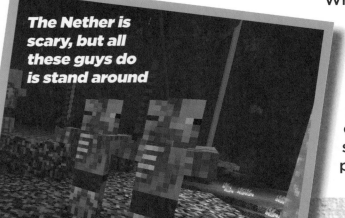

The Nether is scary, but all these guys do is stand around

PORTALS TO ANOTHER WORLD

Let's be honest, few of us built a Nether portal without looking it up. Not many people would think to mine a very difficult to (safely) find block, place them together in a certain way, then use fire on them.

Whether or not you were told how to do it, there's nothing like building your first portal, activating it and stepping through to see what's on the other side. So many pigmen...

BRILLIANT Minecraft BUILDINGS

The smaller of the two boats!

CRUISE SHIP
Poncharelli's Cruise Ship is massive and full of detail. You start on an island in the captain's house, and signs direct you to cross the water to the nearby cruise ship. Once there, you'll find everything a holidaymaker could want – over 100 guest cabins, 20 crew rooms, suites for more important crew members, a theatre, restaurant, swimming pool, gift shop and much more!

The ballroom area

The diner area

THE LORD'S CASTLE

The creator of this map, Marinclaric, says that he built it in just one month! It's based on a medieval castle and features both the main building, grounds and utility buildings, all surrounded by the castle walls. Inside you'll find a throne room, teleportation room and two rollercoasters. There's even a fully working ecosystem, meaning that you can play on Survival mode and get everything you need to live without ever leaving the walls. Amazing!

FUNLAND

Built by SuperP, this map would take days to fully explore. It features over 100 different attractions, including rollercoasters, log flumes and water rides! There are 17 restaurants, seven shops, rides designed for young children and much more. There are even secret sections to find, which reveal the history of Funworld and the people who built it. Proof that no matter what you imagine, you can build it in Minecraft if you put in the time!

The castle drawbridge and interior gardens

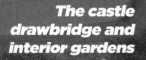

A rooftop garden

SUN CITY

Luca Borges based Sun City on Brazilian cities like São Paulo and Goiânia, but this map is recognisable wherever you are in the world. The city is huge, with a mix of skyscrapers and street-level buildings, two parks, homes and condominiums, and even restaurants and shops. All you can do is explore, but there's a huge amount to do. There's even an out-of-town village area to find! It's not the first city built in Minecraft, but you can see the care and attention that has gone into it.

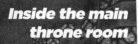

Inside the main throne room

CONTINUED ON PAGE 54

43

DESIGN YOUR NEXT MINECRAFT BUILD!

Before you build something new in Minecraft, it's worth planning it out first. Use this grid to design a new Minecraft creation then, once you've worked out what you want, go and make it in the game!

46

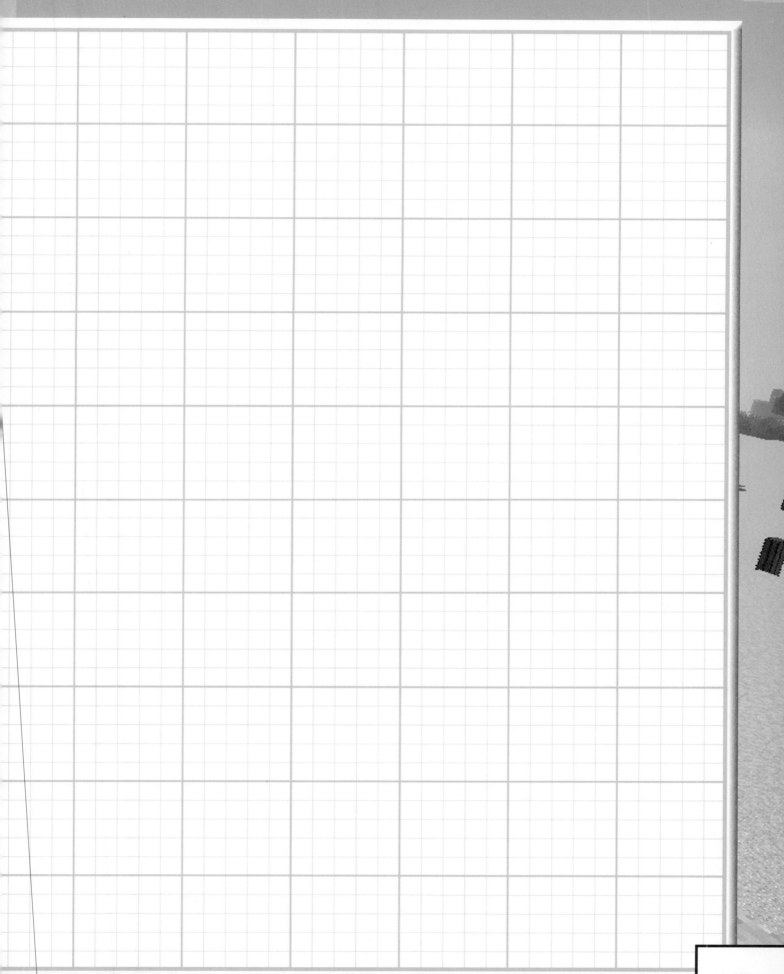

MINECRAFT JOKES

Reckon you've got any Minecraft funnies that are better than these? We suspect you have!

DID YOU HEAR ABOUT THE MINECRAFT MOVIE?
It was a blockbuster!

WHY ARE THERE NO CARS IN MINECRAFT?
Because the roads are always blocked off!

WHERE DO GHASTS LIVE?
The Nether-lands!

WHY DOESN'T MINECRAFT COME WITH A MANUAL?
Because the developers had writer's block!

HOW DO STEVE AND ALEX GET THEIR EXERCISE?
They go for a run around the block!

DID YOU HEAR ABOUT THE CREEPER'S BIRTHDAY PARTY?
It was a blast!

HOW DO MINERS PICK THEIR NOSE?
With a pickaxe!

WHY IS THIS THE LAST JOKE?
Because it's the ender-the-page!

101 THINGS YOU NEVER KNEW ABOUT MINECRAFT

57

Wear a pumpkin mask for seasonal fun – and protection!

Pumpkins can be worn as helmets! Just drop one in the "helmet" armour slot. Wearing a pumpkin on your head restricts how much you can see, but it also stops endermen from noticing you at night!

58

A suit of chainmail armour. Draughty!

Chainmail armour can't be crafted (only traded for or dropped by mobs), but you can repair it using iron ingots on an anvil. Chainmail armour is slightly weaker than iron armour, but stronger than gold.

59

Water helps you get up and down easily

Going up and down stairs can be slow, so why not use water? If you jump into water you won't be hurt by your fall, and if you let water flow down a long drop you can use it to swim up and down more quickly.

60

An enchanted book, caught while fishing

Your fishing rod may catch treasure and junk. Treasure includes enchanted books and name tags, while junk includes damaged boots and rotten flesh to more useful things like string, bottles and bowls.

61

A witch hut with a cauldron, crafting table and flower pot

Witch huts are the only place where flower pots and cauldrons are generated. Neither is hard to make, but if you're trying your best to scavenge items rather than build them, this is the place to look!

62

A redstone fuse helps you keep your distance from TNT

Setting a block of TNT alight can be a risky thing to do, but you can use redstone to create a fuse so that you don't have to get too close. When you're ready, connect up a redstone torch, then run!

63

An eye of ender showing which direction to go

When you craft an ender pearl with blaze powder it creates an eye of ender. When you throw an eye of ender, it flies in the direction of the nearest stronghold, leading you to the end portal!

64

Golden swords aren't much good in a long fight

Golden swords are incredibly weak, but enchant easier than any other weapon. If you add the looting enchantment, you don't even need to use the sword to feel its effects – just carry it!

65

Obsidian makes a fantastically damage-resistant building material

Obsidian has a strong blast resistance, so you can use it to build walls that protect you even if creepers explode close by! It can only be destroyed with a diamond pickaxe or the wither's blue wither skull attack.

66

Even this underground man-made pool can be fished in

You can fish deep underground, but you'll have to make sure you've got a lot of time free. If you fish in water that isn't exposed to the sky, it will take a lot longer to catch something – almost twice as long in fact!

67

The mushroom Island biome is free from hostile mobs!

Mushroom island biomes are the only place completely free from hostile mobs. Take as much time as you want to explore, because no enemies spawn anywhere nearby, even underground.

68

Build shortcuts through the Nether - if you're brave enough!

You can build shortcuts through the Nether by creating a new portal back to the Overworld. Every block you move in the Nether matches eight in the Overworld, so you can get around quickly!

69

Butchers will trade meat with you

Pay attention to the profession of villagers you're trading with. Butchers buy and sell meat, and librarians buy and sell books. Whether you're after items or emeralds, you have to trade with the right villager!

70

You need Nether wart to create awkward potions

If you want to brew potions, you'll need to collect Nether wart from inside a Nether fortress. This creates an awkward potion as a base for better ones, otherwise you'll only be able to make potions of weakness.

71

Mining ore with silk touch means you can reuse it as decoration - like this lapsis lazuli ore

The silk touch enchantment allows you to collect blocks that would otherwise drop items when mined – for example, various types of ore or non-standard types of dirt.

72

Use water to clear grass and collect seed easily

You can use water to clear long grass quickly, with the added benefit that it will cause grass seeds to drop and wash them all into one place for easy collection!

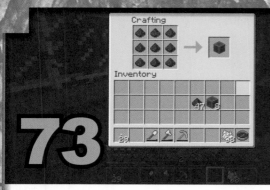

73

Redstone crafts into redstone blocks

Some resources, like redstone dust, coal, clay and snow, can be crafted back into blocks (and then back into resources), which means you can carry nine times as much in a single inventory slot!

74

Use a bucket on a cow for free milk!

You can milk cows with an empty bucket. You can then craft the milk with eggs and wheat into cake, or drink it to recover from poisoning and other status effects. Keep a milk bucket with you if you fight a witch!

75

Use an anvil to combine items with enchanted books

You can transfer the enchantment on books to any valid item using an anvil. An anvil also lets you repair enchanted items without losing the enchantment, so it's worth having one around!

76

Wild ocelots can be tamed into cats

You can tame wild ocelots by feeding them fish, but they're hard to get near – move carefully, hold out the food and wait for the ocelot to come to you. When you tame it, it will become a cat with a new skin!

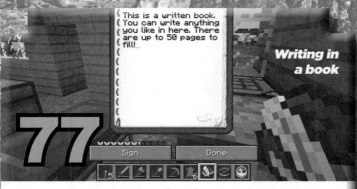

77

Writing in a book

You can create books then write in them. This is useful for sharing information or keeping notes on your progress in worlds, so you know what you were doing and where you're going when you come back!

78

Mobs can open these doors, so take care!

Pressure plates are a great way to make a simple automatic door, but remember that mobs can activate them as well, so be careful – you don't want your doors to let through zombies!

THE FINAL PART IS ON PAGE 70!

BRILLIANT Minecraft BUILDINGS

MODERN MANSION

Minecraft makes it easy to create things that look rustic, but what if you want to make something more modern? Well, user Yo Dawg has created this mansion based on the latest architecture and fashion trends. Search the grounds to find a hot tub, swimming pool, roof garden and fountain. It looks more authentic if you download and install the Modern HD texture pack!

The mansion grounds

A swimming pool. Anyone for water polo?

A stylish, modern lounge

MOUNTAIN SKY VILLAGE

This map was built by a pair of users - qwerti10 and McBreakdown – who used it on the CubCon Server Network. This village exists on the side of a cliff, and every house is connected through a network of hidden paths and tunnels within the landscape. It's a very scenic map, and one of the biggest we've featured, so make sure you've got a decent PC to look at it! Take your time and see what fun stuff you can find, like the water wheel we stumbled across!

PRODIGIOUS CITY

It might look like just another city map, but Prodigious City was designed by a team of people (led by SimJoo) and, if you look closer, you'll notice that it's full of landmarks from around the globe! Bridges, skyscrapers, parks and more. Around the city, you'll find pixel art, jumping puzzles, a huge mining system and even a map of the city to find your way around. There's enough city here to keep you and your friends occupied for hours!

Giant living areas protruding from cliffs

Passages weave in and out of the rocks

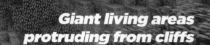

CASTLE SPEIRE OF AERITUS

If you like Medieval-style builds, this creation of KCRafted will blow you away. Castle Speire of Aeritus is a world built around a huge, incredibly detailed castle in the European style. Around it, you'll find a church, a market square, tall towers, and ships of all kinds, from galleons and sloops to fictional airships and blimps. A truly stunning piece of work. It seems almost impossible to imagine that someone built this, and even harder to imagine ever seeing it all!

The village stretches far into the distance

10 AMAZING COMPUTERS AND DEVICES BUILT IN MINECRAFT

With the right resources and enough imagination, it's possible to build just about anything in Minecraft! Here are some of our favourite builds!

10

Animal Cannon

We're not sure how useful this is, but it looks like a lot of fun to play around with. YouTube user Kiershar has created his own animal cannon, which is capable of flinging a pig so far that it can never be found. The ingenious design uses a tower packed full of TNT to launch an animal in a minecart clear across the game map. "Pig and the minecarts were never seen again," Kiershar wrote after a test launch. "I've walked for a few Minecraft days in the direction of the launch, with no success. It's time to call off the search. RIP pig."

www.tinyurl.com/TenBuilds1

Automated Chicken Farm

Creating a plentiful source of food is key to survival in Minecraft. But instead of harvesting food, how about creating an automated chicken farm? Player Data has done just this – he has built a huge facility where caged chickens lay eggs, which hatch into chicks, then are cooked with lava blocks when fully grown!

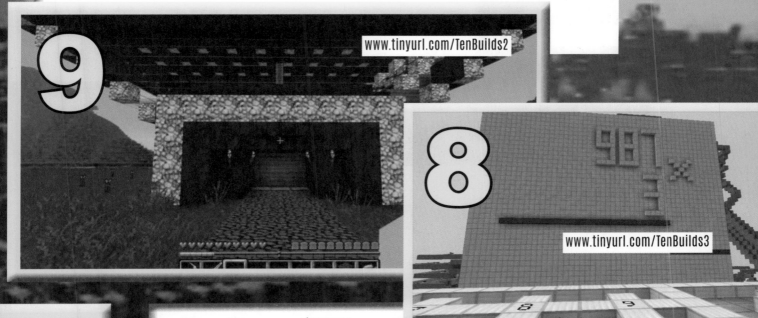

www.tinyurl.com/TenBuilds2

9

8

www.tinyurl.com/TenBuilds3

Scientific Calculator

Need a device that can help you with some tricky sums? Check out this remarkable build from 16-year-old MaxSGB. His scientific calculator can display 25 digits, and its 14 functions include multiplication, division, addition and subtraction. The calculator is complex and huge – all told, it takes up five cubic metres!

Word Processor

So you have a calculator for maths, but what if you need to do some essay writing in Minecraft? Clever user Koala Steamed has you covered with his fully working word processor, which has a keyboard, display and even a save function!

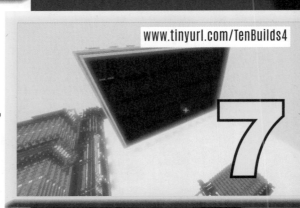

www.tinyurl.com/TenBuilds4

7

CONTINUED OVER THE PAGE!

57

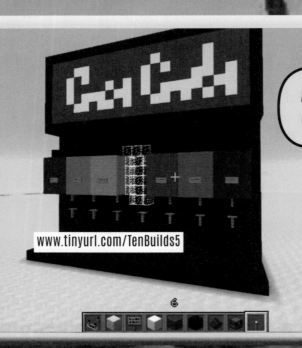

www.tinyurl.com/TenBuilds5

6

Soda Machine

Life can be tough in Minecraft, but having a luxury like a drinks machine would make things more fun, wouldn't it? Prolific Minecraft builder SethBling has created one that dispenses drops of potion (with names like Choka-Cola and Dr Sprinter) and even chunks of ice!

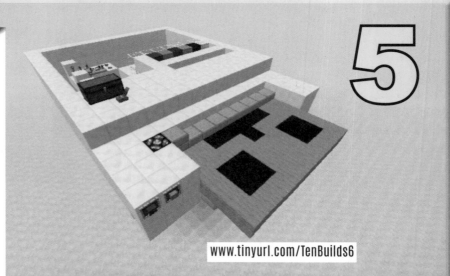

5

www.tinyurl.com/TenBuilds6

Printer

Now this one really is clever! You start by placing coloured blocks in a large chest to create a picture, then YouTube user ACtennisAC's printer creates a full-scale version of that image. To demonstrate, he draws a creeper face with lime and black wool. When he has finished, he closes the chest and the printer gradually recreates the image out of large woollen blocks!

4

www.tinyurl.com/TenBuilds7

Grabber Machine

Another creation from SethBling, this is a simulation of one of those grabber machines where you try to pick up a stuffed toy with a wobbly metal claw. But because this is Minecraft, you control the grabber by stepping on pressure plates, and the items inside include creepers, witches and ocelots. Okay, so they aren't great prizes, but at least it doesn't eat up all your change!

www.tinyurl.com/TenBuilds8

3

Playable Guitar

Only a giant would be able to pick up FVDisco's colossal six-string guitar, but thanks to a clever system of pressure pads you can program it to play a series of individual notes or even entire chords – just like a real guitar! The same user has also created a programmable piano, which is capable of playing surprisingly complex classical music.

Piston Elevator

There are lots of ways to create lifts that make getting to higher places easier in Minecraft, but few are as sophisticated as Cubehamster's redstone elevator. Capable of sending you to the top of a 14-floor building in seconds, it's equipped with switches and doors that only open when the lift has stopped moving. Colourful and compact, it's a masterpiece of Minecraft design!

www.tinyurl.com/TenBuilds9

2

Redstone Computer

A few decades ago, the tech behind this computer would have been cutting edge. But user LPG has spent the last two years building a computer inside Minecraft. It's one of the most sophisticated we've seen in the game. You can play noughts and crosses and a trivia game on it, and it comes with its own wireless keyboard and mouse! LPG's adding to it all the time too – a recent update shows the machine browsing the web.

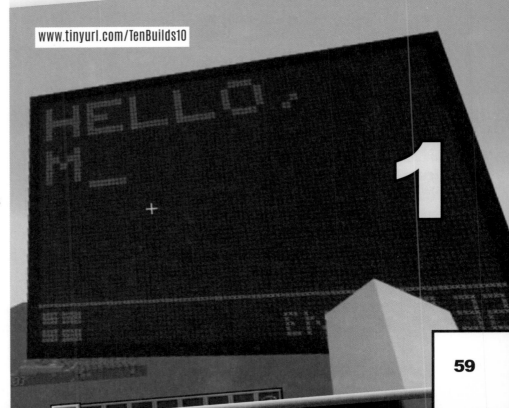

www.tinyurl.com/TenBuilds10

1

59

MAKE YOUR OWN
MINECRAFT
CAKE!

Get creative and bake your very own delicious Minecraft cake, following our simple step-by-step instructions!

Making a cake in Minecraft is pretty easy. You just need three milk, three wheat, two sugar and an egg, with the milk on the top, the wheat on the bottom and the sugar and milk in the middle. For that, you'll get seven slices of cake and three empty milk buckets to reuse later. It looks tasty, it fills up your hunger bar and it's one of the few Minecraft foodstuffs you can put out on a table when you've got friends coming round!

It looks so tasty that you couldn't be blamed for wanting to eat it in the real world. Of course, making Minecraft's cake in the real world is a little different. The wheat (okay, flour), eggs and sugar are all still vital, but you'll need a couple of extra ingredients, and an oven instead of a crafting table.

So what does it take to make that cake a reality? We find out!

WHAT YOU NEED
- Rolling pin
- Wooden spoon
- Mixing bowl
- Sieve
- Scales
- Kitchen mixer (optional)
- Knife for spreading
- Tin foil
- 2 x 21cm by 21cm tins greased with a little bit of butter (or use one tin twice)
- Ingredients
- 450g (16oz) softened butter
- 450g (16oz) caster sugar
- 8 large eggs
- 450g (16oz) self-raising flour
- 4 level tsp baking powder
- Jam (apricot for preference)
- Ready-roll white icing
- Red sugar paste

PLEASE GET HELP FROM A PARENT OR GUARDIAN BEFORE TRYING THIS RECIPE!

GETTING STARTED

MAKING THE SPONGE

● You can make this cake as either a single sponge or a Victoria sponge sandwich. This recipe is for a sponge sandwich, but for a slightly easier cake you can simply halve all the ingredients and apply the icing when the cake is cool.

● If you want to make the sponge sandwich but don't have two identical cake tins, you can always cook the sponges one after the other.

1. First, pre-heat the oven to 180 degrees.

2. Cream the butter and sugar together until they're pale and fluffy. Add the first egg and stir it thoroughly into the mixture, before adding the next one. Continue until all the eggs are in the mixture.

3. Sieve the flour and baking powder into the mix before stirring together with the wooden spoon. (Continued over the page!)

Pour into the greased cake tins, using the wooden spoon to make sure the mixture reaches all the corners, and flatten the top.

If you're using silicone cake tins, place them on a baking tray to provide a bit of extra stability as you take them in and out of the oven.

4. Put the cake tins in the oven, and check back after 10 minutes to see if the cake tops are brown. Once they are, cover the tops with foil and place back in the oven for another 25 minutes (although your oven may take more or less time to cook).

5. You'll be able to tell if the cakes are cooked by putting a toothpick into a cake and pulling it out. If the toothpick comes out clean, they're ready! If there's cake mix on there, put the cakes back in the oven for a little bit longer.

6. When they're done, leave the cakes out until they've cooled completely.

MAKING THE SANDWICH

● If you're making your cake into a Victoria sponge sandwich, now is the time to put the two halves of your cake together.

● Wait for the cakes to finish cooling, then turn the first cake tin upside down onto a board. Spread a thick layer of jam over the top. Tip the second cake out onto a board, and place it on top of the jam.

DECORATING THE CAKE

1. Put a thin layer of jam over the very top of the cake. This will be the glue that holds the icing onto the cake.
2. Lay out the ready-rolled icing and cut a straight line down each side to make the circle into a square. Go along each side of the square, cutting small rectangles out of the edge to make the zigzag pattern along the edge of the icing.
3. Dust the kitchen surface with icing sugar. Take the red sugar paste and roll it out flat over the icing sugar, then cut four large and four small squares out.
4. Carefully lower the white icing square over the cake so that the zigzag pattern is draped around the sides. Then place the red squares onto the top, trying to match the pattern on the top of the cake in the game. And you're done!

How to be a MINECRAFT EXPERT

One of the great things about Minecraft is that it's easy to start playing, but it can take years to master it completely! If you want to play like a Minecraft pro, you need to know the tricks and secrets the experts use in every situation. That's why we've got a genuine Minecraft genius to share their advice on all sorts of things!

Keep a bed with you and the nights are no trouble

These horses will be useful later

Expert Exploring

Exploring your Minecraft world is a big part of the fun, but it's quite dangerous if you lose your way, run out of tools or don't make it home before nightfall!

Expert players know to plan for these occasions. Take fresh tools with you and a bed so you can skip nights by sealing yourself in a small bunker. Make sure there's enough light so mobs don't spawn! You can then pick up the bed and use it the next night.

Experts also know to take a boat in case there's water to cross. Not only is it fast, it also doesn't deplete your hunger bar, which is important! The best way to explore is on horseback. Note where you see any horses and return there once you get a saddle. Horses can move quickly, which hugely expands your range and makes it very difficult for mobs to kill you!

Expert Mining

Some blocks, like diamond and emerald ore, are very rare, while others can be collected only with the right tools. An expert will keep more than one set of tools in their inventory so that they can switch to the right one for any situation.

Gold tools enchant more easily than other kinds, so if you have a pickaxe with the looting enchantment, only use it when you find a rare type of block so that you get as much as possible out of it. The same goes for a shovel or pickaxe with the silk touch enchantment.

Rare ores often spawn near lava, so if you're mining them you have to be careful. An expert will first mine around the blocks to ensure the resources the blocks drop don't fall into the lava and get incinerated! You can also protect yourself by standing in a pool of flowing water.

If you're searching for resources, beginners dig randomly into cliffs, but experts know just where to look. You can usually find coal, iron, redstone, diamond and lapis lazuli ores between 5 and 15 blocks above the bedrock, so start there. You can maximise the blocks you see by digging 1x2 corridors with a two-block gap between them.

Break out the gold tools!

Stand in water to keep yourself safe near lava

At the right level, you'll find several types of rare ore

If you hit bedrock, you're too low to find lots of ore

You don't have to keep looking at a map to fill it –just once in a while!

Maps even fill up if you're below ground

Expert Mapping

Did you realise that you don't have to hold onto a map all the time? Keep it in your quickbar and switch to it for a few seconds every now and then, and you'll still fill it up but won't slow yourself down. Perhaps the best expert tip for map-makers is that you can make maps of the surface even when you're underground. This means if you're wandering around a cave system, you can explore two parts of the Overworld at once! Finally, when you finish a map, make a copy by crafting it with an empty map, so you always have a finished version even if you die.

Expert Farming

Expert farmers know that crops don't necessarily need sunlight to grow. If you place torches or glowstone around your crops, they'll grow even at night!

Experts also plant crops in rows, because crops grow more quickly if they're planted next to a crop of a different type!

Breeding animals is easy if you learn the food they eat, and you can use it to lead them around. If you're building a herd to breed animals for resources, hold the food in your hand and they'll follow. Rabbits and pigs follow carrots, cows, mooshrooms and sheep follow wheat, and chickens follow seed.

Use torches or glowstone to keep crops growing at night

Plant crops in rows and they'll grow faster

66

Pile the items correctly, and when you remove this pickaxe...

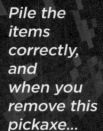

... you can instantly craft a spade!

Expert Fighting

When you fight an enemy, they briefly flash red to indicate that a hit has landed. While this is happening, they can't take any more damage, so if you hammer the attack button your weapon will take damage even though it's not causing any harm. Experts know to attack slowly and deliberately, ensuring every weapon lasts as long as possible! You can also make sure you land a critical hit by jumping at an enemy and pressing attack just as you hit the high point of your jump. Critical hits cause the most damage and, if you use this technique, you'll ensure they always land.

Expert Crafting

Why not try and make multiple items on a single crafting grid? The recipes for an iron pickaxe and iron shovel overlap: put down two sticks instead of one in each slot, then one iron on the left, two iron in the middle and one iron on the right. Remove the pickaxe. You'll have the recipe for a shovel left there!

On a PC, holding down Shift when you remove an item from the grid makes as many as you can. So if you place enough resources onto a grid straight away, you can create up to 64 of most items in a click.

Mobs can't be hurt while they're red

Critical hits make stars appear when they land

BRILLIANT MINECRAFT GOODIES!

Minecraft has grown into something far, far bigger than a video game! You can now buy all sorts of Minecraft goodies!

CLOTHES!
There are lots of different choices when it comes to cool Minecraft T-shirts. You can get baseball caps, hats, socks and hoodies too!

YOUR OWN STEVE HEAD!
Ever, er, wanted to look like Steve?! Well you can actually buy yourself a big cardboard Steve head if you really want to! This one really made us laugh!

YOUR OWN CREEPER!
How about this? Your very own Minecraft creeper! It will put any other cuddly toys you have to shame! Oh, it makes an exploding noise too. BOOM!

OFFICIAL ACTION FIGURES!
You can get a range of Minecraft action figures, including Steve, Alex, a zombie and an enderman! Each one comes with its own accessory!

NIGHT LIGHT!
Who needs a boring bedside lamp in their bedroom? Especially when you can get this brilliant light-up block of redstone ore instead! We love it!

FOAM SWORD!
Believe it or not, you can get official Minecraft tools and weapons – not that you can do any damage with them, thank goodness!

LEGO MINECRAFT!
There are lots of LEGO Minecraft sets to choose from – The Farm, The First Night, The Cave, The Ender Dragon and a Crafting Box – and more on the way!

PART FOUR

101
THINGS YOU NEVER KNEW ABOUT
MINECRAFT

79

An ender portal with all of its eyes inserted

You need to insert 12 eyes of ender into an ender portal to activate it. They all have at least one already there, but remember eyes of ender have a chance of breaking when thrown, so you'll need more than 11!

80

An arrow leaving a critical hit trail

If you fire an arrow at its full strength, it leaves a trail of stars. If you see this, you know it will do a critical hit when it lands, inflicting the most amount of damage on mobs!

81

All three types of prismarine. Remember you can't mine it!

Prismarine only appears in ocean monuments and is hard to mine. Unless you have a silk touch pickaxe, it will shatter into prismarine shards when it breaks.

82

Sit, Ubu, sit. Good dog.

If you walk too far away from your tamed wolf, it will automatically teleport near to where you are, so you don't need to worry about losing it in the middle of a fight!

83

A savanna village at night

At night, some villages get dark enough for mobs to spawn. You may want to add more lighting to try and keep them from killing the inhabitants or accidentally blowing them up!

84

A pig with a saddle, and one without

You can ride pigs and horses, but only with a saddle. You can tame horses so that they obey your commands, but pigs will wander aimlessly unless you use a carrot on a stick to direct them.

A mooshroom in the mushroom biome

85

Mooshrooms are a type of cow that spawns in mushroom island biomes. Use a bowl to milk mushroom stew out of them or, if you need milk, shear the mushrooms off them, which turns them back into regular cows.

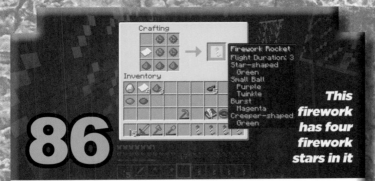

This firework has four firework stars in it

86

If you want to, you can load multiple firework stars into a single firework. They'll all explode at the same time, so make sure you're not looking the other way when they go off!

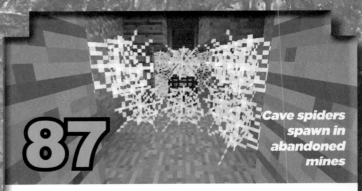

Cave spiders spawn in abandoned mines

87

Cobwebs can be turned into string if you break them with a sword or shears. Abandoned mines are a good place to stock up. Just don't break your sword, as you'll eventually run into a spider-spawner!

A zombie-proof bunker is ideal for nighttime safety!

88

Zombies are attracted to wooden doors, and on harder difficulty modes can break through them. Protect yourself by using steel doors. Zombies can't get in and other players have to use a button to open them.

You can use golems to distract the wither

89

The wither attacks any mob it sees, so if you're trying to kill it, create a distraction by first building several golems. They won't do much damage to the wither, but they can draw its fire while you get in close!

90

Ender crystals in the End

In the End, there are large obsidian pillars topped with ender crystals. When the ender dragon gets close, they recharge its health, but if you destroy one while it's being healed it will lose a chunk of health!

91

Abandoned mines are normally full of rails you can use

Abandoned mines appear almost anywhere underground and are the only place to find minecarts and rails. The amount of rails is normally huge, so stock up, as it's quicker than crafting them.

92

You can grow a giant jungle tree this way

You can grow giant trees like jungle trees and dark oak easily enough. You need to plant four saplings together, and then make sure that you fertilise one of them with bone meal.

93

You can dye clothes to change their colours

Crafting leather armour (clothes) with dye changes their colour. You can dye clothes several times to create different shades of each colour. Dip them in cauldrons to remove the dye completely!

94

As you can see, trees need a lot of space to grow!

With enough space and light, you can grow trees underground planted on dirt – a great way to keep a supply of wood underground. When you cut down a tree, it drops saplings that you can immediately replant!

95

This painting shows you how to summon the wither!

Whenever you place a painting, it selects a random image. Some are references to classic games like Donkey Kong, Grim Fandango and International Karate+, and one hints at how to summon the wither!

96

Fishing during a rainstorm. Don't catch a cold!

If you fish during a rainstorm, it decreases the time you wait to get a bite. You can make five catches in the time it takes to make four when not raining. The block you're fishing in has to have rain land on it!

97

These eight maps have been placed together to make one big map!

If you make lots of maps using the same scale, you can then place them in item frames next to each other. When you do that, you then make one giant seamless map!

98

You can dye some animals, like sheep!

Rather than dyeing wool blocks, dye a sheep. You need one unit of dye to colour a block of wool, but the same amount of dye colours a whole sheep, which drops up to three blocks of wool when you shear it.

99

Where running water meets flowing lava, you get cobblestone - not obsidian!

Lava and water do odd things when they meet. Running water turns still lava into obsidian. Running lava turns still water into stone. And if lava AND water are both running, they turn into cobblestone.

100

The golden treasure of an ocean monument!

Inside an ocean monument, you'll find a large room with a huge prismarine pillar. This is the treasure chamber, and there are solid gold blocks that you can collect as a reward for defeating the monument!

101

Two chickens on a lead

Leads let you drag mobs wherever you want, but don't think you have to do one at a time. You can connect a lead to a mob for every space in your quickbar, which means you can take up to nine with you!

CELEBRITIES WHO LOVE MINECRAFT!

Loads of people love playing Minecraft, including these famous faces!

MILA KUNIS

Movie star Mila Kunis is known for films such as *Oz the Great and Powerful*, *Jupiter Ascending* and *Annie*. Turns out though that she loves her video games too, and has admitted being a Minecraft fan!

JACK BLACK

Jack Black lends his voice to the *Kung Fu Panda* films, and has starred in movies such as *School Of Rock*, *The Muppets* and *Gulliver's Travels*. He has been pictured in a Minecraft T-shirt before, and is believed to be an avid player of the game!

FELICIA DAY

Actress Felicia Day has appeared in loads of films and TV shows, including *Star Wars Detours* and *Buffy The Vampire Slayer*. As followers of her Twitter account - @feliciaday - will know, she loves her Minecraft too!

DEADMAU5

Musician deadmau5 - or Joel Zimmerman, to give him his birth name - isn't just a big Minecraft fan, he has also mentioned it in his music! He has been to the annual Minecon convention too!

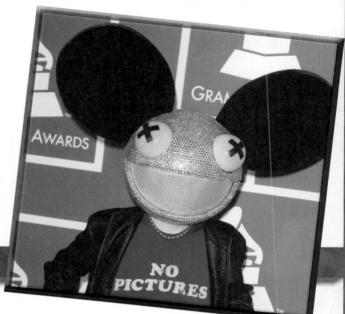

JONATHAN ROSS

Chat show host Jonathan Ross has given Minecraft a go, although he hasn't turned out to be an avid player of the game. His username is WossyMan.

NOTCH

Markus Persson is, of course, the man we have to thank for Minecraft in the first place. It was his brilliant idea, and he's one of the most popular and famous players of the game!

77

78

UH-OH!

Poor Callum! He's been separated from his sword and doesn't know which path he needs to follow! Can you help? The answer is on page 92!

THE BIG Minecraft QUIZ

Chances are, by now you'll know all about Minecraft. So test your knowledge in our quiz! The answers are on page 92!

1
Which of these items can you NOT use as fuel in a furnace?
(A) Coal
(B) A bucket of lava
(C) A stone pickaxe

2
What can you feed zombie villagers to cure them?
(A) A golden carrot
(B) A golden apple
(C) Nether wart

Where do giant mushrooms grow?

3
Giant mushrooms grow naturally in two types of biome. Which ones?
(A) Mushroom island and roofed forest
(B) Mushroom island and taiga
(C) Swamp and jungle forest

4

Which type of armour can't be crafted, only found or traded for?
(A) Diamond armour
(B) Gold armour
(C) Chain armour

5

The tools that work the fastest are made out of
(A) Gold
(B) Stone
(C) Obsidian

Does this wolf need fish to breed?

6

All animals need different foods to breed. Which ones eat fish?
(A) Wolves
(B) Chickens
(C) Ocelots (cats)

7

If you see red droplets coming off a block, that means:
(A) There's lava above it
(B) You can mine it to get redstone
(C) There's water above it

8

Why are compasses useful in Minecraft?
(A) They always point north
(B) They always point to the last place you slept
(C) They always point to your original spawn point

9 Which type of block can you smelt into glass blocks?
(A) Cobblestone
(B) Sand
(C) Gravel

10 Which enemy does NOT appear in the Nether:
(A) Ghast
(B) Blaze
(C) Witch

11 Nether portals need to be built out of a specific block. Which is it?
(A) Diamond
(B) Obsidian
(C) Lapis lazuli

12 What do ender pearls allow you to do?
(A) Fly
(B) Teleport
(C) Breathe underwater

Endermen drop ender pearls, but what do they allow you to do?

13 Wither skeletons use what weapon?
(A) A bow and arrow
(B) A gold axe
(C) A stone sword

14 What's special about Netherrack?
(A) It burns forever if set on fire
(B) It spreads to other blocks
(C) It can't be destroyed

15

What's inside the special beacon block?

What rare item do you need to make a beacon block?
(A) A dragon egg
(B) A Nether star
(C) A firework star

16

How many strongholds does each map contain?
(A) One
(B) Three
(C) Five

17

Horses live in just two biomes. Which ones?
(A) Savanna and plains
(B) Desert and taiga
(C) Jungle and mesa

19

You can wear a pumpkin on your head. But why is this useful?
(A) Its protects you from fireballs
(B) It stops endermen noticing you
(C) It stops golems attacking you

18

Podzol and mycelium are variants of dirt. But what do they allow you to do?
(A) Grow crops faster
(B) Absorb water blocks
(C) Grow mushrooms even in full light

20

Which enchantment allows you to see better underwater?
(A) Respiration
(B) Fortune
(C) Protection

OFFICIAL SKIN PACKS!

Skins change the way your character looks in the game. You could be a superhero or your favourite TV show character!

f you own the PC version of Minecraft, you can take advantage of the many skins that are available online (although make sure you ask your grown-up before you go looking for them!). You used to be out of luck if you were playing on a games console, but now official skin packs have started arriving! Check out some of these!

DOCTOR WHO!

Exterminate! Exterminate! The Doctor has made it into the Overworld, and so far two different packs of *Doctor Who* skins are available!

STAR WARS!

These skins feature characters from the *Star Wars Rebels* TV show. We love the stormtrooper the best!

The Doctor and his sidekick

We love the stormtroopers!

The motley rebel crew!

Just look at those Daleks!

Marvel's mighty Avengers!

If *The Avengers* aren't enough, the *Guardians of the Galaxy*, including Star-Lord, Groot and Rocket, are ready for action!

GUARDIANS OF THE GALAXY!

Look at that cool Thanos skin!

THE AVENGERS!

Minecraft could use some more superheroes! Marvel's mightiest heroes – Iron Man, Captain America and Black Widow – are ready to do battle with some creepers!

THE SIMPSONS!

Bart, Homer, Lisa, Maggie and Marge lead a host of characters from *The Simpsons* who've headed to Minecraft.

CHRISTMAS!

There's already snow in Minecraft, but if you want to feel festive every December, load up the special Christmas skin pack! There's even a creeper with a Santa hat!

Where To Find Them

You can get these packs on Xbox Live or PlayStation Network. Note that not all packs are available for all consoles, and they'll usually cost you a little bit of money, too. Make sure you check with your grown-up before you get them!

CROSSWORD

Can you solve our special Minecraft crossword? Good luck!

ACROSS

5. To write a book in the game, you need a book and....
6. The man who came up with Minecraft!
7. Found in abandoned mineshafts and slows you down!
9. A block that will burn forever when you set fire to it.
10. You use this as electricity.
12. You do this to make the most of the blocks and materials in the game.
13. You need a furnace for this.
15. You need one of these to travel on rails!
16. Craft one of these and you'll be able to sleep!
17. You can use this to repair tools, weapons and armour.

DOWN

1. These are the people you can trade with.
2. A mob that explodes when it gets too close!
3. A cow that you'll only find in the mushroom biome.
4. A boss mob that you'll only find at the End.
8. Jungle, desert and ice plains are all types of this.
11. One of the game modes.
14. A boss mob with three heads.
15. The name of the company that publishes Minecraft.

Can you find the Minecraft words at the bottom in our grid?

P	O	S	B	E	Q	R	F	F	O	D	G	M	S	E	E	R	T	X	Z
E	P	P	L	X	C	Y	T	J	Y	D	N	E	Z	K	B	C	A	O	S
B	J	R	V	X	R	C	S	Z	U	E	W	U	N	X	P	M	E	I	H
S	K	R	O	W	E	R	I	F	W	G	F	M	Q	Y	B	V	K	T	A
A	S	X	W	T	D	P	D	I	H	H	K	S	W	K	K	N	U	Z	P
V	S	T	V	Q	S	R	I	A	Y	W	S	R	E	G	A	L	L	I	V
G	P	R	Q	T	T	E	S	G	V	L	N	K	Z	M	D	K	Z	Q	M
Z	Z	A	K	A	O	T	T	M	S	A	N	Z	C	O	X	B	O	F	K
Q	D	C	I	I	N	C	N	J	E	H	L	J	V	O	H	H	M	O	E
D	B	E	D	X	E	F	E	H	T	L	E	G	E	R	L	F	B	W	R
C	O	N	J	P	F	K	M	M	J	U	O	L	Y	V	I	B	I	D	T
Z	B	I	G	C	T	C	T	R	S	M	H	G	T	S	C	E	E	I	H
J	H	M	X	M	G	F	N	T	Q	F	M	U	T	E	S	H	S	A	Y
J	F	K	F	N	O	G	A	R	D	R	E	D	N	E	R	Q	L	M	X
C	O	E	G	O	O	Q	H	R	J	V	F	D	M	V	E	X	L	O	K
T	O	V	F	F	J	P	C	M	C	L	I	Y	H	Q	H	A	U	N	M
E	H	U	Q	S	P	S	N	Y	O	E	P	W	V	B	T	X	A	D	C
C	H	N	I	P	G	L	E	O	X	B	N	U	O	R	M	C	M	S	K
T	N	S	T	O	L	E	C	O	E	R	S	I	O	C	V	I	P	A	X
W	J	D	D	I	X	U	E	B	V	K	S	P	M	J	N	P	I	B	I

WORD SEARCH

MINECRAFT
BLOCKS
ZOMBIES
PIGS
FIREWORKS
GHAST
TREES

ENCHANTMENT
DOGS
OCELOTS
SHELTER
PORTAL
MINECART
REDSTONE

DIAMONDS
MOBS
VILLAGERS
GOLEMS
BED
ENDERDRAGON
LAVA

The Amazing A-Z of MINECRAFT

A is for ARMOUR

You'll find five kinds of armour in Minecraft – diamond is the strongest, leather is the weakest!

B is for BLOCKS

Minecraft is built on blocks! Glass is the weakest, bedrock is the strongest.

C is for CREEPERS

Creepers have a horrible habit of sneaking up behind you and going boom!

D is for DIAMOND

The strongest ore that you can turn into tools!

E is for ENDER DRAGON

The boss you need to kill if you want to win the game!

F is for FARM

The perfect place to grow your own food!

G is for GOLEMS

These are special utility mobs that you can use to fight enemies on your behalf!

I is for INVISIBLE

One of the game's most useful potions – make sure nobody can see you!

K is for KEYBOARD SHORTCUTS

If you play Minecraft on a PC, you can do some things more quickly with your keyboard!

M is for MOBS

Mob is short for mobile, and is used to describe the moving computer-controlled creatures in the game.

H is for HUNGER

In Survival mode, you need to make sure you're eating enough – you don't want to run out of hearts!

J is for JUNGLE

One of the game's biomes, and one that holds many secrets, such as temples and rare items.

L is for LAVA

Lava is dangerous, but it's a great source of light and can set things on fire.

 **is for NOTCH**

Notch is the other name for Markus Persson, and he's the man who invented Minecraft in the first place!

 **is for ONLINE**

If you play Minecraft on the PC, you can go online and join in some massive multiplayer games!

 is for PIG

Did you know you can ride on pigs in Minecraft? It's fun! But you'll need a carrot on a stick and a saddle if you want to!

 **is for QUILL**

Get a quill and a book, and you can write down things in the game itself!

 is for REDSTONE

Minecraft's very own version of electricity!

 **is for SKINS**

How your character looks in the game can be changed by making them a new skin!

T is for TNT

TNT is a block that explodes, but it needs to be activated by something like redstone or fire!

U is for UPDATES

Especially on the PC, Minecraft is continually evolving. Always be on the lookout for fresh official updates to download!

V is for VILLAGE

This is where you'll find Minecraft NPCs (non-playable characters) living.

W is for WITHER

The wither is an undead boss that shoots exploding skulls.

X is for XBOX AND PLAYSTATION

There are some amazing skin packs available too for the Xbox 360, Xbox One, PlayStation 3 and PlayStation 4 versions of the game!

Y is for YOUTUBE

There are so many amazing Minecraft YouTube videos – we've talked about some of them on page 36!

Z is for ZOMBIE

A zombie is a hostile mob that comes up to you and punches you! Charming!

ANSWERS!

Did you manage to solve the puzzles we set you throughout this book?
Here's where you can check to see just how well you did!

MAZE

CROSSWORD

VILLAGE
QUILL
MOOSHROOM
ENOTCH
CREEPER
COBWEB
BIOME
NETHERRACK
ENDERDRAGON
REDSTONE
SURVIVAL
CRAFTING
SMELTING
WITHER
MINECART
MOJANG
BED
ANVIL

WORDSEARCH

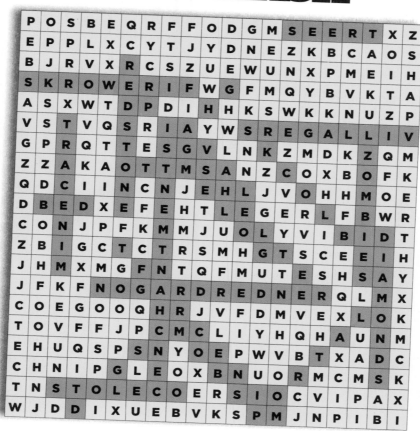

P	O	S	B	E	Q	R	F	F	O	D	G	M	S	E	E	R	T	X	Z
E	P	P	L	X	C	Y	T	J	Y	D	N	E	Z	K	B	C	A	O	S
B	J	R	V	X	R	C	S	Z	U	E	W	U	N	X	P	M	E	I	H
S	K	R	O	W	E	R	I	F	W	G	F	M	Q	Y	B	V	K	T	A
A	S	X	W	T	D	P	D	I	H	H	K	S	W	K	K	N	U	Z	P
V	S	T	V	Q	S	R	I	A	Y	W	S	R	E	G	A	L	L	I	V
G	P	R	Q	T	T	E	S	G	V	L	N	K	Z	M	D	K	Z	Q	M
Z	Z	A	K	A	O	T	T	M	S	A	N	Z	C	O	X	B	O	F	K
Q	D	C	I	I	N	C	N	J	E	H	L	J	V	O	H	H	M	O	E
D	B	E	D	X	E	F	E	H	T	L	E	G	E	R	L	F	B	W	R
C	O	N	J	P	F	K	M	M	J	U	O	L	Y	V	I	B	I	D	T
Z	B	I	G	C	T	C	T	R	S	M	H	G	T	S	C	E	E	I	H
J	H	M	X	M	G	F	N	T	Q	F	M	U	T	E	S	H	S	A	Y
J	F	K	F	N	O	G	A	R	D	R	E	D	N	E	R	Q	L	M	X
C	O	E	G	O	O	Q	H	R	J	V	F	D	M	V	E	X	L	O	K
T	O	V	F	F	J	P	C	M	C	L	I	Y	H	Q	H	A	U	N	M
E	H	U	Q	S	P	S	N	Y	O	E	P	W	V	B	T	X	A	D	C
C	H	N	I	P	G	L	E	O	X	B	N	U	O	R	M	C	M	S	K
T	N	S	T	O	L	E	C	O	E	R	S	I	O	C	V	I	P	A	X
W	J	D	D	I	X	U	E	B	V	K	S	P	M	J	N	P	I	B	I

QUIZ ANSWERS

pickaxes don't burn!
apples have a healing effect.
mushrooms can also grow in swamps, but only in Pocket Edition!
armour can't be crafted by the player!
tools destroy blocks very quickly, but have low durability.
es will eat fish, but it doesn't make them breed!
and water drips through blocks, but water drops are blue!
passes always point back to the very start.
olestone smelts into stone, and gravel won't smelt at all!
ches only appear in the overworld.
d a portal frame out of obsidian, then set it on fire to activate it.
y teleport to wherever you throw them!
mal skeletons use bows, but Wither Skeletons carry stone swords!
etherrack keeps burning until you intentionally put it out.
Nether Star. You have to kill The Wither to get one.
ere are only ever three strongholds on every map!
orses live on Savanna and Plains, and nowhere else.
ese blocks keep mushrooms alive.
umpkins block your view, but hide you from Endermen!
Respiration. It also lets you breathe underwater for longer.

SCORES

0-4: Wood: Don't worry, you'll learn more Minecraft facts as you play!

5-9: Stone: A good start. You can probably tell the difference between iron ores and iron doors!

10-14: Iron: Not bad at all! Spend some more time in the Nether and you'll be an expert soon.

15-19: Gold: There's not much more we can teach you. Have you visited the End yet?

20: Diamond: Great job! The Ender Dragon probably didn't even see you coming!